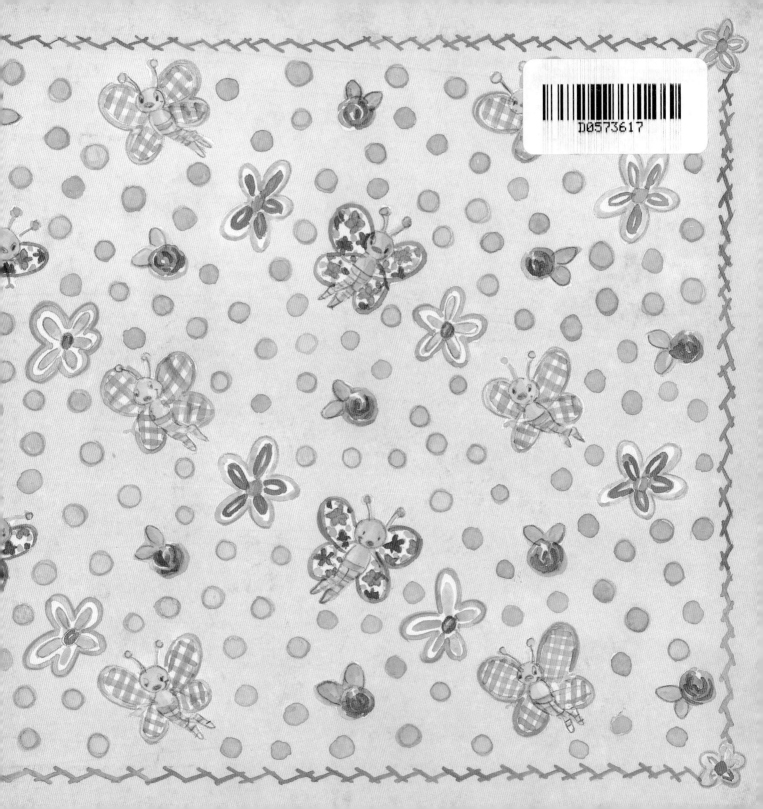

This book belongs to Princess:

_____

who loves it very much!

Designer: Celina Carvalho
Production Manager: Colin Hough-Trapp

Library of Congress Cataloging-in-Publication Data:
Finsterbusch, Monika.
Princess Lillifee's secret / by Monika Finsterbusch.
p. cm.
Summary: When Clara the fairy is told that she is too little to perform magic,
Princess Lillifee decides to become her teacher.
[1. Princesses–Fiction. 2. Fairies–Fiction. 3. Magic–Fiction. 4. Friendship–Fiction 5.
Animals–Fiction.] I. Title.
PZ7.F49856Prs 2006
[E]–dc22
2005027843

Text and illustrations by Monika Finsterbusch
● 2005 Coppenrath Verlag GmbH & Co. KG, Münster, Germany
All rights reserved.

First published in Germany under the title *Prinzessin Lillifee hat ein Geheimnis*
English translation copyright ● 2006 Harry N. Abrams, Inc.

Printed and bound in China
10 9 8 7 6 5 4 3 2 1

HNA
harry n. abrams, inc.
a subsidiary of La Martinière Groupe
115 West 18th Street
New York, NY 10011
www.hnabooks.com

Princess Lillifee's Secret

by Monika Finsterbusch

Abrams Books for Young Readers
New York

One spring day, Princess Lillifee sat down by a little creek to write invitations to her Butterfly Ball.

All of a sudden, she saw a bottle sparkling in the water, and she heard a voice say, "Please–let me out!"

Lillifee grabbed the bottle and held it up. She couldn't believe her eyes– Bella, the little fairy, knocked against the glass from inside.

Lillifee removed the cork, and the little creature flew into the air. "Bella, what are you doing in there?" Lillifee asked.

"Do you promise not to get mad? Cross your heart?" Bella said.

"Cross my heart," Lillifee said.

"And you won't tell my magic teacher, Jasper?"

"I won't."

"I was trying out a new spell during magic class, and I accidentally conjured myself into this bottle," the little fairy answered. "I'm just no good at magic. Everyone says it's because I'm too small to do spells."

"That's not true!" Lillifee exclaimed. "If you like, I will teach you magic, and at my Butterfly Ball you can show everybody how good you can be. But you'll have to stay hidden until the ball so that your spells will be a surprise. And I know just where you can stay!"

"No one will find you in the attic. But be careful, because my mouse friends Clara and Cindy are very curious."

Over the next few days, Lillifee spent every minute she had in the attic . . .

. . . teaching Bella spells.

They also had fun making cake . . .

. . . and playing
dress-up.

After a while, Lillifee's friends became curious. "I don't get it," Henry the rabbit said. "Lillifee's always busy. What's going on?"

"She's probably preparing for the Butterfly Ball," Pugsy the pig said.

"But why not include us in her plans?" Carlos the frog said. "I think it's something else."

Clara and Cindy, the two mice,
decided to follow Lillifee.

The mice followed the princess into the attic.

"I can hear Lillifee's voice!" Cindy whispered.

"Who is she talking to?" Clara asked.

"I can't see. Let's come back tomorrow while Lillifee is in school."

The next morning, Clara and Cindy dug through the whole attic, and
they found . . .

"Bella!" the mice cried.

"Why are you hiding?" the mice peeped.

Bella told them her story. Clara and Cindy laughed.

"You're too little to go to magic school!" Clara said.

"I'm not so little!" Bella responded. "And I can do magic."

"Prove it," Cindy said.

Bella marched outside and the mice followed. Along the way, they called for the rest of the animals to join them.

"All right," Bella said. "I will now transform you all into little princes. Hobus, schokus, filikus, three times pinky-cat!"

In a sudden gust of thunder and lightning, all the animals were hurled into the air. But something wasn't right. Bella groaned and put her head in her hands. "Lillifee, help! Help!" Bella shouted.

"What did you do?" Lillifee said. She closed her eyes and murmured, "Mumi, mami, mimi, mauz, four times white raven-thunder!"

"Hurray! It worked!" her friends shouted.
"It's lucky I came home from school in time," Lillifee
said. "But where's the little magician now?"

They found Bella behind a tree.

"I'm so ashamed," Bella said. "I've done everything wrong again. I was just trying to show you that little fairies can do magic, too."

"Mistakes happen to every fairy," Lillifee said. "It has nothing to do with your size! Dry your eyes and come with me. I have a surprise for you."

"Hocus, malocus, eight times elephant-geiser!" Lillifee shouted. Suddenly a castle appeared. It was just the right size for a little fairy such as Bella and was a perfect place to practice magic—and to stay out of trouble!

Over the next few days, when Lillifee wasn't preparing for the Butterfly Ball, she helped Bella with her magic.

The Butterfly Ball began with Bella's performance. In front of all the guests, she took a deep breath and said, "Hobus, schnurpsus, flatterus, ten times colorful-mix!"

A thousand glittering butterflies came out of her magic hat and filled the air! The guests applauded enthusiastically.

Bella heard a voice she recognized. "Bravo! Bravo! Wonderful!"

"I invited your teacher, Jasper, and told him that you have become a real magic fairy," Princess Lillifee explained.

"Lillifee was right," Jasper said, bowing to the princess. "You may be small, but you are a very talented fairy!"

Jasper bowed to Bella, and all the guests let out a cheer. Bella thanked Lillifee for training her in secret. "Thanks to you, now I know that size isn't as important as hard work and good friends!"